Charlie's Key

by

JOHN HARRIS

Illustrations by

Tom Morgan-Jones

notreallybooks

Charlie's Key
First published 2006 by
notreallybooks
Suite 111 Dorset House Chelmsford Essex CM1 1TB
Reprinted 2010

ISBN 0-9552129-0-1

ISBN 978-0-9552129-0-1

John Harris would like to thank the following :
Tom Morgan-Jones, Sabrina Scolaro,
David Rees and the staff and pupils,
past and present,
of St. Cedd's School, Bradwell on Sea

British Library Cataloguing in Publication Data:
a catalogue record for this book is available from the British Library

This edition printed 2010 by The Lavenham Press

For Andrea and Francesca

Chapter One

Charlie lived with his mum in a small house in a village by the sea.

At the end of Charlie's road was the beach, which always seemed to be bright and sunny in the summer, and cold and windy in the winter.

In the middle of the village was the green, which had a pond with ducks on it, and around the green was a church, a pub, a shop with a Post Office, and the school that Charlie and all his friends went to.

It was a small village, and a quiet one. Not much ever happened, and apart from what you'll read at the end of this story there's nothing very unusual about the place.

One day, when Charlie was in year five, he got home from school to find his mum in the kitchen looking very pleased with herself. "Guess what?" she said, "I've got a new job!"

"Great!" said Charlie, "Well done!"

"There's one slight problem, though," she said. "The job's not in the village, it's in town, so I'll have to drive, and you know what the traffic can be like sometimes."

"Terrible!" said Charlie. His mum nodded.

"So there might be times when I get stuck in traffic on the way home," she continued, "and if that happens you'll get home before me."

"But I haven't got a key!" said Charlie.

"Aha!" His Mum smiled as she put her hand in her pocket. "You have now!" And she held up a shiny new front door key.

"Oh, wow!" said Charlie.

"Now listen," she said as she handed it to him. "I want you to be sensible and grown up about this."

"I will be!" said Charlie.

"If I'm not here when you get home then just let

yourself in. If you have homework then do that first, then you can watch TV or read a book."

"Okay!" Charlie was grinning with excitement.

"Don't bring any of your friends home with you," his Mum went on, "'cos you'll get silly and that's when accidents happen."

"I won't."

"And don't make yourself a cup of tea or something to eat in case you spill hot water or cut yourself. I won't be long, so just wait for me."

"Okay!"

"And if there's a problem go next door to Mrs Taylor, she's going to to keep an eye on you."

"Okay!" said Charlie.

"And one more thing: don't lose your key, will you?"

"Oh, Mum," he said, "I'm not stupid!"

Chapter Two

So the next day Charlie went to school with his key for the first time. He didn't want to lose it in the playground while he was playing football, so to keep it safe he put it in his pencil tin.

He also thought it would be more grown up of him not to tell everyone he had a front door key. So he didn't tell anyone. He didn't even tell Jamie, the best friend he sat next to in class.

They always had Maths to begin with, so Charlie put his pencil tin out on the table and got on with his project.

After a while Jamie groaned and said, "Oh, no! I've left my pencil sharpener at home! Can I borrow yours?" And without waiting for a reply he opened Charlie's tin. "What's this?" he asked, picking up the key.

"My key," said Charlie.

"Oh, wow!" said Jamie, "Have you got a front door key?" Then he held the key up and whispered loudly "Look everybody! Charlie's got his own key!"

Well, honestly! The way the whole class behaved you'd think they'd never seen a key before! Within seconds it was being passed around the class from one person to another under the tables so Mr Rees couldn't see what they were up to.

Jamie passed it to Francesca, who passed it to Emma who gave it to Amos who gave it to Andy who passed it over to Richard's table and when it had been all around that table it was passed to Daisy's table and then to Catriona's and then to Khatun's and then to Vicky's and then over to Harry's.

Charlie wasn't happy about this. He was trying to keep an eye on it so he knew where it was and who had it. The last thing he wanted was for someone to lose it, and when Ross finally passed it back he breathed a sigh of relief and put it safely in his pocket.

By break time the whole school seemed to have heard about Charlie's key, and they all gathered around him in the playground.

"Let's have a look!" someone asked.

"Give it here!" said someone else.

"Can I see?"

"Pass it here!"

"Oh, wow!"

Once again, everyone wanted to have a look and everyone was passing it to everyone else. Even the little kids in Year One wanted to see it.

Then along came Claudia, who sometimes forgot her manners. "Let's have a look!" she said as she snatched the key.

It was one of those awful moments when everyone could see what was going to happen, but no-one could do anything about it. As Claudia snatched the key it seemed to slip from her fingers and fly up into the air.

There was a horrible silence as everyone watched Charlie's key fly across the playground and then start to fall down, down, down and then land through a grate into the drain.

Weeeeeeee

        eee

         eeeeeee

             Plopp!

"Oh, brilliant!" said Charlie.

"Oh, no!" Everyone else said as they pointed to the grate, "You've lost your key, Charlie!"

"Yeah, I can see that," said Charlie, "Thanks, Claudia!"

Claudia shrugged. "It was an accident - sorry!"

Poor Charlie! Claudia was right - it was an accident, he knew, but that didn't make any difference. His Mum had told him not to lose his key and he'd gone and lost it on the first day he had it and, boy, was she going to be cross!

He worried about it for the rest of the day and there was nothing anyone could do, or say, to make him feel better. It was like a big dark cloud that hung over him for the rest of the day.

As he walked along his road he could see there weren't any lights on in his house and his mum's car wasn't there. 'Oh, no,' he thought, 'she's not back from work yet!' And Mrs Taylor's lights were off as well - she was out too!

He wondered what to do. He thought about going to Jamie's but then realised that if he went to Jamie's his mum wouldn't know where he was when she did get home so she'd be worried. She was going to be cross when she heard about the key and he didn't want to make things any worse! All he could do was sit on the doorstep and wait for her to get home, so that's what he did.

He didn't have to wait very long before he saw his mum's car coming down the road and he began to feel better, even though he knew he was going to be in trouble.

"What happened?" she asked when she saw him on the doorstep, "did you forget your key?"

"Er, no," he said. "I'm afraid it, er, fell down a drain. Sorry!" He smiled hopefully.

"Oh, dear!" she said. "Never mind, I'll just have to get you another one tomorrow."

"You're not cross?" he asked.

"No, 'course not!" she smiled. "I'm sure it was an accident. Accidents happen!"

Phew! He was so relieved that she wasn't cross with him. "Thanks!" he said, "I promise I'll look after the next one!"

When Charlie got home from school the next day his mum had his new key ready for him. It was exactly the same as the first one except that she'd tied a length of string through the hole in this one so that it could go around his neck.

"There!" she said as she dropped it over his head and tucked it under his shirt. "Keep it around your neck and under your shirt and you won't lose it!"

"Brilliant!" he
said. "You're the best mum in
the world!" He took the key out
to have one more look at it
and then he dropped it back
under his shirt and, apart from
when he went to bed or had to have a wash, the
key stayed around his neck for the rest of the
year, right up to the summer holidays.

Chapter Three

At the beginning of year 6, Charlie got a place in the school football team. He was really excited and his mum was very proud of him.

There was a real buzz of excitement in the changing room when the team were getting ready for the first match of the season. Mr Church, the team coach, came in to check they were all ready.

"Okay, boys?" he asked.

"Yes, Sir!" they all answered. Then he saw Charlie and said "Oh, Charlie! You'd better not leave your key around your neck during the match in case you fall over and it pokes you in the eye!"

"I didn't think of that!" said Charlie.

"Take it off and leave it somewhere safe," he said, "I'm locking the changing room door so it'll be alright in here."

"Okay!" said Charlie. So he took the key from around his neck and then carefully wrapped the string around and round and round the key so it was like a neat little ball.

Then he looked for somewhere to hide it. He needed somewhere safe, somewhere where no-one would find it, somewhere where no-one would even think of looking for it. Then - AHA! - he found somewhere, a brilliant place where no-one would ever find it! He hid the key and went out to join the others on the pitch.

The match was a good one and Charlie's team won 2 - 0 and Charlie nearly got a goal in the second half but it just hit the post. After the match they were all in the changing room getting dressed and feeling very pleased with themselves. They were laughing and joking and talking about the match when, just as he was putting his shoes and socks on, Charlie suddenly remembered his key.

But he couldn't remember where he'd put it! He looked all around the changing room but he couldn't find it anywhere. He knew he'd put it somewhere really safe, somewhere where no-one would think of looking for it. And that was the problem: he'd put it somewhere so safe, where no-one would even think of looking for it, that even he couldn't think where that was!

He looked under all the benches in the changing room: nothing. He looked in all the open lockers: not there. It was just while he was climbing onto a bin to look on top of the lockers that Mr Church walked in and said "Charlie, what on earth are you doing?"

"Looking for my key," he called across the changing room. "I put it somewhere safe, like you said, but I can't remember where!"

"Okay everybody!" Mr Church clapped his hands to get everyone's attention, "can you all help Charlie look for his key, please?"

Everyone looked for Charlie's key. They searched the floor, the lockers, the showers and everyone's boots and bags. They even checked the window ledge that was so high up Jamie had to climb on Harry's shoulders to look, but it wasn't there either. Wherever it was, Charlie had put it in such a clever place that no-one would ever find it!

"Are you sure you had it, Charlie?" Harry asked.

"Yes!" Charlie said. "It was round my neck and I took it off!"

"So where did you put it when you took it off?"

"If I knew that I'd know where it was!" Charlie snapped.

"Are you sure you haven't swallowed it?" Jamie asked. Everyone else thought that was funny, but Charlie didn't.

They couldn't find it anywhere. One by one they gave up and went home, leaving Charlie hoping his mum was home by now.

But she wasn't.

As he walked towards his house he could see the lights were off and her car wasn't there and Mrs Taylor's lights were off so she wasn't home either. Once again, all he could do was wait.

 When his mum got out of her car she saw him sitting on the doorstep. "Where's your key?" she asked. Charlie shrugged. "I don't know. Mr Church said I should take it off for the match and put it somewhere safe, which I did. But now I can't remember where I put it, and because it was such a good place to hide it no-one can find it!"

"Oh, you ninny!" she laughed. "Not to worry! How did the match go?"

"We won two-nil and I hit the post!"

"Well done!" she said. "That's more important. We'll get you another key tomorrow."

"You're not cross with me?" he asked.

"No, don't worry," she said, "these things happen!"

Chapter Four

By now you can probably guess what Charlie's mum did the next morning: she got him another key. But this time she also got a really clever key ring for it to go on. It was a very powerful spring with a clip at both ends. The key went onto the clip at one end and the clip at the other end fastened to the belt loop of Charlie's trousers. Then the key hung down beside his waist and when he needed to open the door all he had to do was pull the key up to the door, turn it in the lock and then let go and the key would spring back to his waist again.

'Brilliant!' said Charlie when they'd hooked it up to his trousers. 'I can't possibly lose this one!'

But there were a couple of problems with the new key ring which he didn't discover until the next day: the first was that when people saw the key dangling beside him on the spring they all thought it would be a bit of a laugh to stand next to him, take hold of the key and then pull it as far as they could before letting go:

THWANNNNGGGG!!!!!

The key sprang back to Charlie's waist really quickly. "Ow!" he said, rubbing his side, "That hurts!" Which, was, of course, the worst thing he could have said because it made everyone want to do it! People sneaked up to him all day to stretch the spring and then let go.

It happened in the playground:

THWANNNNGGGG!!!!!

"Ouch! That's not funny!" he said.
But everyone else thought it was.

In assembly:

THWANNNNGGGG!!!!!

"Ouch!!!!!"

"Ha! Ha! Ha!'

In the dinner queue:

THWANNNGGGG!!!!!

"Stop it!!!!"

"Ho! Ho! Ho!'

Even when he was sitting quietly at his desk trying to work, people would find an excuse to walk past his table and twang the key.

THWANNNGGGG!!!!!

"Ouch!!!!!"

Mr Rees looked up from his marking and said "Charlie! Work quietly, please!"

"Sorry!" he said.

But a minute later it happened again.

THWANNNGGGG!!!!!

"Ouch!"

"Charlie!" Mr Rees looked over at him rather sternly.

"Sorry!" Charlie smiled at him.

At home time Charlie was happy to walk home alone because it was the first bit of peace he'd had all day. But when he got to the front door he found the second problem with his new keyring: as soon as he put the key in the door and turned it in the lock the spring started to work, just as it was supposed to. But because the key was in the lock the spring couldn't pull it back to Charlie's waist, so instead it pulled Charlie towards the door.

THUUNNNKKKK!!!!!

"Ouch!" he said as his nose hit the door just as it opened and he tumbled in to the house.

Once he was in the house he had other things to do so he forgot about it - until the next time he had to use his key and the same thing happened again.

THUUNNNKKKK!!!!!

"Ouch!" he said as his nose hit the door.

In fact every time he used his key the spring would pull him right up to the door and

THUUNNNKKKK!!!!!

he'd hit his nose on it and go tumbling in as the door opened.

By the end of term he'd almost got used to bashing his nose on the door and it didn't even seem to hurt as much.

On Christmas morning he found a stocking at the bottom of his bed, and at the bottom of the stocking was a big bright blue electric toothbrush. 'Oh wow,' thought Charlie, 'I might enjoy cleaning my teeth for a change!'

That night he was looking at himself in the bathroom mirror as the toothbrush buzzed over his teeth and he thought his face looked different somehow. It was another minute or two before he realised why: his nose was changing shape and getting flatter at the end from being bashed on the door!

Chapter Five

Christmas came and went and, as always, the holidays were over too quickly. On the first day back at school Jamie asked Charlie if he'd like to go to his house for tea the next day.

"Yeah, that'd be great!" said Charlie. "Thanks!"

"It might not be great," Jamie warned him.

"Why not?" asked Charlie.

"Two reasons," Jamie replied. "Firstly, my mum bought way too much Christmas food this year, and secondly someone bought her a toasted sandwich maker!"

"What's wrong with that?" he asked.

"You'll see tomorrow!" Jamie said.

And when he got to Jamie's the next day Charlie saw exactly what he meant. Jamie's mum was trying to use up all the left over Christmas food and for tea she'd made them toasted Christmas Cake sandwiches.

"Mmmm, it's, er..... unusual!"
Jamie told his mum as they
chewed the first
mouthful.

"Very nice!" said
Charlie,
who knew it would
be rude to say anything
else. He ate it as quickly
as he could.

"Gosh! That was
quick!" said
Jamie's Mum.
"Would you like
another?"

"Er, no thanks! I think
I've had enough now
thank you!"

Charlie smiled at Jamie's mum while Jamie was
pretending to be sick behind her back.

"It's a good idea to leave room for something else," she said, "I've baked you boys a cake!"

She certainly had. It was a Victoria sponge sandwich, one of those cakes where you bake two halves separately and then put them together with jam or cream in the middle. But this one was different. This one had cranberry jelly in the middle and brandy butter on the top!

As soon as he finished a slice Charlie could feel his stomach starting to protest. It started to rumble and gurgle like washing machine.

As soon as he thought he could go home without seeming rude he thanked Jamie's mum for inviting him and said it was time for him to go.

"Are you sure you've had enough to eat?" she asked.

"Yes thanks!" said Charlie, "I'm quite full, thank you!"

"Do you want another piece of cake to take with you?" she asked.

"No thanks," he smiled, "I think I've had enough now!"

"Well don't worry!" she said, "this sort of cake keeps for ages in a tin so there'll be a piece waiting for you next time you come." She and Jamie waved goodbye as Charlie walked off down the road, and he wondered if he'd ever dare to go to Jamie's house again.

Chapter Six

When Charlie got to the top of his road he could see

his mum wasn't back from work yet.

He walked down the road towards the house and

then

Whoa!!!!!!!!!

stopped dead in his tracks.

Sitting on his doorstep was the biggest,

    longest,

      widest,

        fattest,

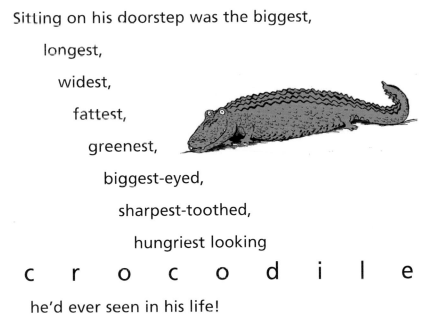

          greenest,

            biggest-eyed,

              sharpest-toothed,

                hungriest looking

c   r   o   c   o   d   i   l   e

he'd ever seen in his life!

A Crocodile?

Charlie wondered what on earth a crocodile was doing sitting on his door step. There weren't any zoos nearby, and there hadn't been a circus in the village for ages, and circuses don't have crocodiles anyway, so where on earth had it come from?

The only explanation he could think of was that this crocodile had swum all the way over from wherever crocodiles lived, taken a little stroll through the village and then stopped for a rest on his doorstep.

'But why mine?' he asked himself.

He also wondered what he should do.

'I know,' he thought, 'I'll nip to the shop and buy some sausages. If he's still here when I get back I'll go: 'Here, crocodile, fetch!' and throw them down the road so he chases after them and that'll give me chance to get into the house!

Yeah! Brilliant!'

But then he remembered he'd been to Jamie's for tea so it was later than usual. The shop would be closed by now.

Then he thought perhaps he should go back to Jamie's and tell Jamie's mum. But then he remembered there was a piece of cranberry jelly and brandy butter cake waiting for him at Jamie's and he decided he'd rather face the crocodile than have to eat another piece of that cake.

He looked to see if Mrs Taylor was in, but - surprise surprise! - all her lights were out. He'd have to deal with the crocodile himself.

Slightly nervously, he smiled at the huge green creature. "Excuse me," he said in his politest voice, "but this is my house and I need to get inside. So if you don't mind I'm just going to reach over you and open the door."

He took hold of the key and reached towards the lock, but as he did so the crocodile SNAPPed his jaws and Charlie leaped back out of the way. The key sprang back to his waist as he did so and Charlie checked his fingers and thumbs. They were all there. He'd stepped back just in time and the crocodile had missed!

Now it seemed that the crocodile was looking at Charlie with more interest. Even though it was beginning to get dark Charlie could see the glimmer of his sharp white teeth.

He took hold of the key again. "Look, I'm sorry about this," he said to the crocodile, "but I really do need to get into this house!"

He reached up to put the key in the lock and again the Crocodile's jaws SNAPPed. Charlie leaped back just in time and the key sprang back to his waist.

He quickly checked his fingers and thumbs - all present and correct.

It might just have been Charlie's imagination, but he was beginning to think the crocodile was looking hungry.

Then he had an idea. 'I know what I'm doing wrong,' he thought, 'I'm being too polite! It's because I'm talking to him that he knows what I'm going to do. If I don't tell him what I'm doing I might get the door open before he knows what's happening!'

So without saying anything else to the crocodile, he reached across to put the key in the lock as quickly as he could.

Again the jaws SNAPPed and Charlie let go of the key and leapt back just in time. He still had all his fingers and thumbs when he checked, but this time the crocodile had the key clenched between his teeth!

For a split second the two of them looked at each other as the spring was stretched between them.

Then, before Charlie could think what to do next, the spring started to work and the crocodile was suddenly pulled towards him and then the spring

went **THWANNNGGGG!!!!!**

The crocodile flew into the air and was thrown right

across the village.

weee

eeeee

eeeee

splat!

Charlie couldn't see, of course, but the crocodile

had landed right in the middle of the village pond.

'Wow!' thought Charlie, 'I just got rid of a crocodile!'

He was feeling really pleased with himself until he

realised that he didn't have his key. The spring was still

there, hanging loosely by his waist, but there was no key

on the end of it. The crocodile must have bitten right

through the spring and swallowed the key!

Charlie had got rid of the crocodile, but he couldn't

get into his house. So, once again, all he could do was

sit on the doorstep and wait for his mum.

Chapter Seven

When his mum got home she got out of the car and saw him sitting on the doorstep. "Oh, Charlie," she sounded tired, "where's your key?"

He shrugged his shoulders. "A crocodile got it."

"Oh yes? Very funny!" His mum laughed as she locked the car door, "where is it really?"

"Honestly! A crocodile got it."

"No, come on," she said, "what happened?"

"Really! A crocodile swallowed it!"

She looked at him for a moment and frowned. "What's the matter?" she asked. "I won't be cross, just tell me what happened."

"That is what happened! A crocodile got it!"

"Listen, Charlie," she said. "I'm not going to be cross with you, but tell me what happened!"

"As far as I know it's been swallowed by a crocodile!" he said.

"Alright," she sighed, "I'm not cross yet, but I'm going to be! Now tell me: where is your key?"

"A crocodile got it!" He was almost shouting.

"Oh, for goodness' sake, this is ridiculous! I will ask you once more: where - is - your - key?"

"A Croco -"

"Listen," she interrupted him, "I've had a long day and I'm tired. Just tell me the truth or there'll be trouble."

They looked at each other and Charlie could see she meant it. But what could he do if she wouldn't believe him? He couldn't tell her a lie.

"You want to know what happened to my key?" he asked.

"Yes." she said.

"You want the truth?" he asked.

"Yes!"

"The absolute truth?"

"Yes!!"

"The complete truth?"

"Yes!!!"

"The honest truth?"

"Yes!!!!"

"The total truth?"

"Yes!!!!!"

"The one hundred per cent truth?"

"Yes!!!!!!"

He took a deep breath and then asked "You want to know the absolute, complete, honest, total, one hundred per cent truth about what happened to my key?"

" Y E S S S S S S S ! ! ! ! ! ! ! "

Now it was her turn to almost shout.

"Okay!" He took another deep breath and began to explain. "I went to Jamie's for tea and when I got home there was a huge crocodile just sitting there – "

"Right, young man, that's IT!" she yelled. She unlocked the door with her own key and pointed upstairs. "Go to your room NOW!"

"Huh?" he protested. "It's not bed time!"

"It is for you, young man!"

"But I haven't had any supper!"

"And you won't get any until you decide to tell me the truth!" They looked at each other for a moment. "Do you want to tell me the truth?" she asked. He opened his mouth to speak but then she added "WITHOUT saying the word 'crocodile'!" He closed his mouth and went straight up to his room.

The last thing he had to eat that day was Cranberry Jelly and Brandy Butter cake, which went round and round his stomach and kept him awake half the night.

The next morning his mum was still in a bad mood. She hardly said a word at breakfast, and when he tried to explain she said she never wanted to hear the word 'crocodile' again. Ever.

He went off to school feeling rather sorry for

himself, but she stayed at home because it was her day off. She did some housework and later in the morning she went to the village shop.

Most of the people who lived in the village seemed to be in the shop and they were all talking about one thing: there was a crocodile in the pond. No one knew where it had come from, or how it got there, and no-one knew what to do with it.
When she heard all this Charlie's mum realised he'd been telling the truth after all.

And so this story has a happy ending, because from that day on Charlie always told his mum the truth, and his mum always believed him.

And if you ever go to that village you'll see a little white fence around the pond, with a sign on it that says:

Please do not feed the crocodile

and you don't see many of them,

do you?